Ladybird books are widely available, but in case of difficulty may be ordered by post or telephone from:

Ladybird Books – Cash Sales Department Littlegate Road Paignton Devon TQ3 3BE
Telephone 01803 554761

A catalogue record for this book is available from the British Library

Published by Ladybird Books Ltd Loughborough Leicestershire UK
Ladybird Books Inc Auburn Maine 04210 USA

Don't Worry William

by Christine Morton
illustrated by Nigel McMullen

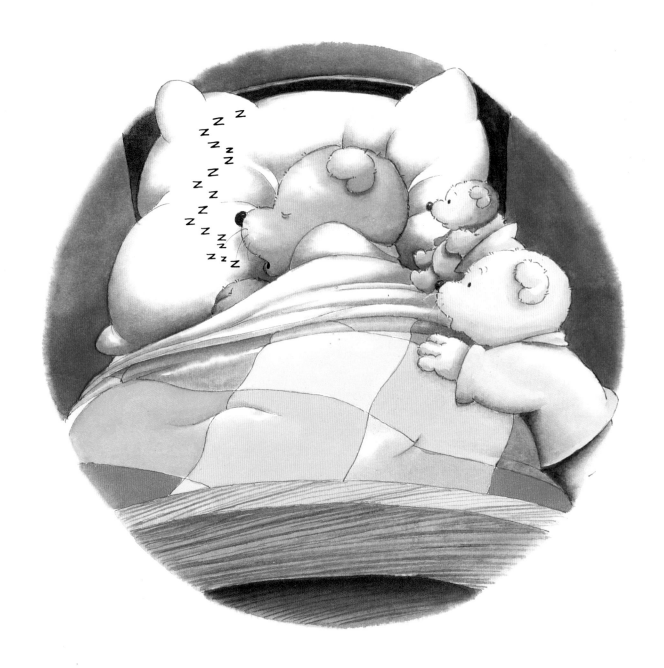

One night, Horace and his teddy bear, William, woke up and decided to be naughty. They waited till Mum was snoring – *zzzzzzzz*. Then they got out of bed. Horace jumped into his monster slippers and the two bears crept downstairs.

Downstairs, it was dark. Sleepy dark.
Creepy dark. In the living room, they heard
a noise. A whispery noise. A crispery noise.
Horace was scared. "Maybe it's a spook!"

"*Tick-tock, tick-tock,*" said the noise.

"Don't worry, William," said Horace.
"It's only the clock!"

Behind the curtain, Horace heard a growl.
A small growl. A yowl-growl. Horace was scared.
"Maybe it's a lion!" he thought.

"*Mee-ow!*" said the noise.

"Don't worry, William," said Horace.
"It's only the cat."

In the kitchen, Horace heard a pop. A soft pop. A bubbly pop. Horace was scared. "Maybe it's a giant frog, gulping in the dark!" he thought.

"Bob, bob, bob," said the noise.

"Don't worry, William," said Horace. "It's only Bob the goldfish, swimming round and round his tank."

Horace and William decided it wasn't so much fun being naughty. They felt a bit wobbly and worried. So they went to find some biscuits, to make them brave.

Horace had *just* got his hands into the biscuit tin when he heard a bang. A Very Loud bang! An On-The-Stairs bang. *BANG, BANG, BANG!*

"There's a th-th-thing!" said Horace. "And it's coming downst-st-stairs!"

They hid behind the settee.

The door opened... *cree-eeak!*

And there stood...
    ...*The Thing!*

The Thing was big. The Thing was cross.
The Thing looked a bit like Mum!
The Thing took a deep breath and said…

"You naughty little boy! Put those biscuits down
and GET UP THOSE STAIRS AT ONCE!"

"Oh Mum," wailed Horace.
"We thought you were a Thing."

Mum put them back to bed.
Back to their big blue bed. Back to their cosy,
dozy cabin bed with no spooky noises.
"Sorry Mum," said Horace.

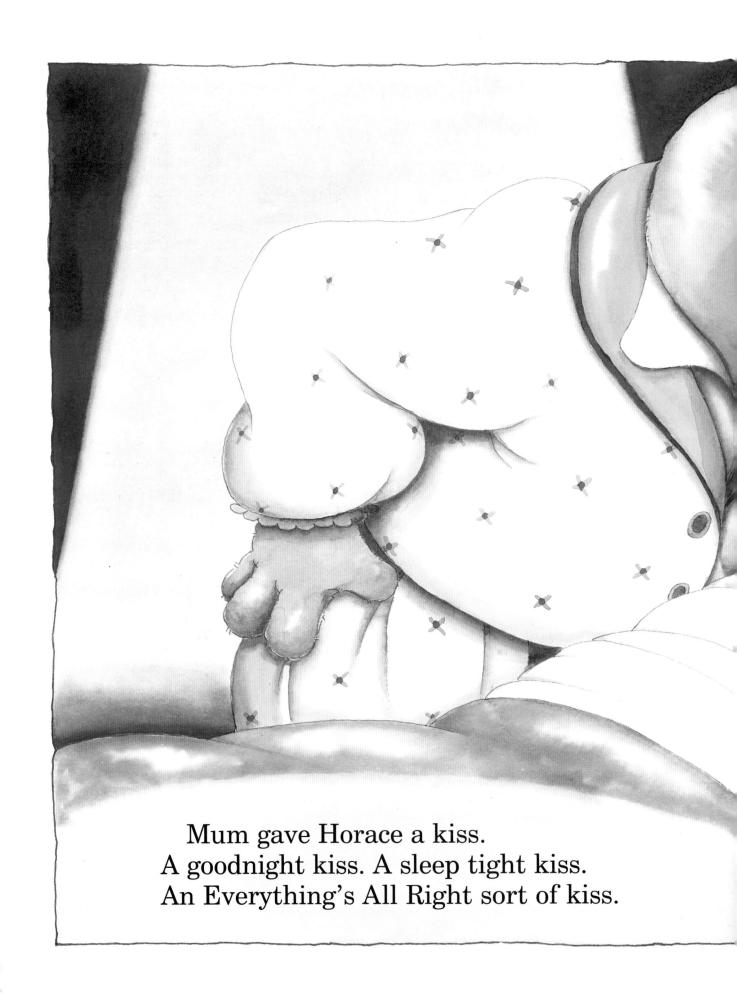

Mum gave Horace a kiss.
A goodnight kiss. A sleep tight kiss.
An Everything's All Right sort of kiss.

Downstairs, the clock went *tick-tock*, *tick-tock*. The cat went *mee-ow*, *mee-ow*. The fish went *bob, bob, bob*.

Upstairs, Horace went *zzzzzzzz*. Mum went *zzzzzzzz*. Even William went *zzzzzzzz*.

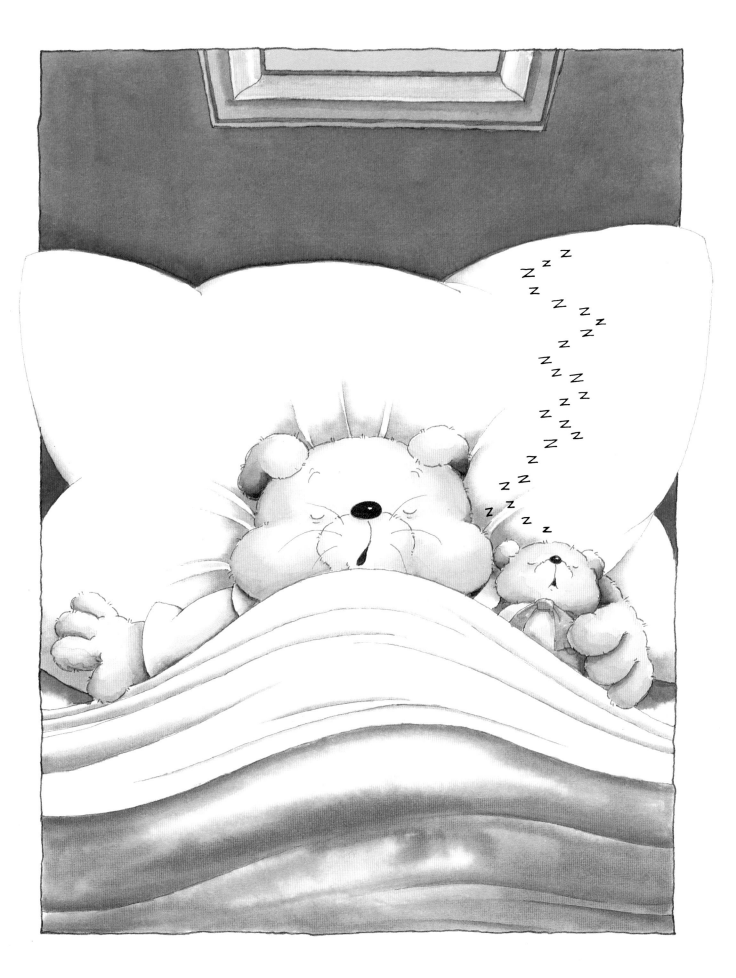

And in the kitchen, a little brown mouse
crept behind the door – and stole the biscuits.

Picture Ladybird

Books for reading aloud with 2–6 year olds

The *Picture Ladybird* range is full of exciting stories and rhymes that are perfect to read aloud and share. There is something for everyone – animal stories, bedtime stories, rhyming stories – and lots more!

Ten titles for you to collect

WISHING MOON AGE 3+
written & illustrated by Lesley Harker
Persephone Brown wanted to be BIG. All she ever saw were feet and knees – it really wasn't on. Then one special night her wish came true. Persephone Brown just grew and grew and *GREW*...

DON'T WORRY WILLIAM AGE 3+
by Christine Morton
illustrated by Nigel McMullen
It's a sleepy dark night. A creepy dark night.
A night for naughty bears to creep downstairs and have an adventure. But, going in search of biscuits to make them brave, Horace and William hear a bang – a very loud bang – an On-The-Stairs bang!
Whatever can it be?

BENEDICT GOES TO THE BEACH AGE 3+
written & illustrated by Chris Demarest
It's hot in the city – *really* hot. Poor Benedict just *has* to cool off. There is only one thing for it, head for the beach – *any* beach! Deciding is the easy part – getting there is another matter altogether...

TOOT! LEARNS TO FLY AGE 3+
by Geraldine Taylor & Jill Harker
illustrated by Georgien Overwater
It's time for Toot to learn to fly, to try and zoom across the sky. First there's take off – watch it – steady! Whoops! Bump! He's not quite ready!
Follow Toot's route across the sky and see if he ever *does* learn to fly!

JOE AND THE FARM GOOSE AGE 2+
by Geraldine Taylor & Jill Harker
illustrated by Jakki Wood
A perfect way to introduce young children to farmyard life. There is lots to see and talk about – pigs and their piglets, cows and sheep, hens in the barn – and Joe's special friend – a very inquisitive goose!

THE STAR THAT FELL AGE 3+
by Karen Hayles
illustrated by Cliff Wright
When a star falls from the night sky, Fox and all the other animals want its precious warmth and brightness. When Dog finds the star he gives it to his friend Maddy. But as Maddy's dad tells her, all stars belong to the sky, and soon she must give it back.

TELEPHONE TED AGE 3+
by Joan Stimson
illustrated by Peter Stevenson
When Charlie starts playgroup poor Ted is left sitting at home like a stuffed toy. It's not much fun being a teddy on your own with no one to talk to. But then – *brring, brring* – the telephone rings, and that's when Ted's adventure begins.

JASPER'S JUNGLE JOURNEY AGE 3+
written & illustrated by Val Biro
What's behind those rugged rocks? A lion wearing purple socks! Just one of the strange sights Jasper encounters as he goes in search of his lost teddy bear. A delightful rhyming story full of jungle surprises!

SHOO FLY SHOO! AGE 4+
by Brian Moses
illustrated by Trevor Dunton
If a fly flies by and it's bothering you, just swish it and swash it and tell it to *shoo!* Trace the trail of the buzzing, zuzzing fly in this gloriously silly rhyming story.

GOING TO PLAYGROUP AGE 2+
by Geraldine Taylor & Jill Harker
illustrated by Terry McKenna
Tom's day at playgroup is full of exciting activities. He's a cook, a mechanic, a pirate and a band leader... he even flies to the moon! Ideal for children starting playgroup and full of ideas for having fun at home, too!